THE CREEPER DIARIES

BOOK SIX

CREEPER ON THE CASE

Also by Greyson Mann

The Creeper Diaries

Mob School Survivor

Creeper's Got Talent

Creepin' Through the Snow: Special Edition

New Creep at School

The Overworld Games

Creeper Family Vacation

Secrets of an Overworld Survivor

Lost in the Jungle

When Lava Strikes

Wolves vs. Zombies

Never Say Nether

The Witch's Warning

Journey to the End

THE CREEPER DIARIES

BOOK SIX

CREEPER ON THE CASE

GREYSON MANN
ILLUSTRATED BY AMANDA BRACK

Sky Pony Press
New York

THE CREEPER DIARIES: CREEPER ON THE CASE.
Copyright © 2018 by Hollan Publishing, Inc.

Minecraft® is a registered trademark of Notch Development AB.

The Minecraft game is copyright © Mojang AB.

Sky Pony Press books may be purchased in bulk at special discounts for
sales promotion, corporate gifts, fund-raising, or educational purposes.
Special editions can also be created to specifications. For details, contact
the Special Sales Department, Sky Pony Press, 307 West 36th Street, 11th
Floor, New York, NY 10018 or info@skyhorsepublishing.com.

Sky Pony® is a registered trademark of Skyhorse Publishing, Inc.®,
a Delaware corporation.

Visit our website at www.skyponypress.com.

10 9 8 7 6 5 4 3 2 1

Library of Congress Cataloging-in-Publication Data is available on file.

Special thanks to Erin L. Falligant.

Cover illustration by Amanda Brack
Cover design by Brian Peterson

Hardcover ISBN: 978-1-5107-3749-5
E-book ISBN: 978-1-5107-3753-2

Printed in the United States of America

DAY 1: SATURDAY

So Mom's on a new kick this month. (Big surprise there, right?)

I guess she signed up for this "Write a Bestselling Novel in 30 Days" class. She says she's finally going to write the mystery that's been burning in her brain for years. Who knew?

Dad got all weird about it. "Maybe you'll be the next Agatha Crispy!" he said—WAY too loudly. That's the famous author whose mystery books are taking over our living room shelves. Maybe Dad's hoping Mom will get rich, like Agatha Crispy. Or maybe he's just glad she's finally over her gardening kick.

Last month, Mom had us eating all these weird vegetables from the garden. Beetroot Soup. Cactus Salad. Stuff that had NO business on our dinner table, if you ask me.

So I decided to jump in Dad's minecart and support this writing thing, too. I figured Mom would be so busy writing, she'd finally stop bugging me about signing up for an extracurricular at school. "Mystery writing?" I said. "Go, Mom! Yeah! Go get 'em!"

I might have overdone it, though, because next thing I knew, she was shoving this book in my face. "If you like mysteries, you should read THIS one," she said.

THE WOLF OF THE BLASTERVILLES

Sherlock Bones

I figured it was an Agatha Crispy book, but it wasn't. It was a Sherlock Bones mystery. Mom's been trying to get me to read those books for ages, but I'm

3

not really into skeleton detectives who ride around on spiders named Dr. Webson. (REALLY???)

Anyway, I dodged that fireball by telling Mom I was WAY too busy writing rap songs to read mysteries. "Maybe Chloe can read it!" I said, tossing the book like a hot potato over Dad toward my Evil Twin.

But Chloe blasted it right back at me. She said SHE was way too busy with Strategic Explosions class. Then she said, "Which extracurricular are YOU signing up for, Gerald?"

CRUD.

Mom started in again, and . . . well, that's how I found myself signing up for the MOB MIDDLE SCHOOL OBSERVER newspaper staff. WHY, you ask? Well, let me tell you. The other extracurriculars at my school are about as much fun as walking across hot lava.

I tried Sprinting class last year, and that was a total bust. I'm not into Spider Riding, Strategic Exploding, or Archery. And I'm REALLY not into Web Weaving or Llama Riding, the two extracurriculars that got added this year. I rode a llama across the desert during vacation last summer (a memory I'd really rather forget), and don't even get me STARTED on how much I hate spider webs. And spiders.

So newspaper reporting didn't sound half bad—especially when Mom said I'd only have to try it for a month. I mean, I'm always writing rap songs. And I'm pretty good at keeping this journal, right? So I decided to crash the newspaper staff meeting after school last Tuesday.

I tried to get my best friend, Sam, to go with me. That slime is usually up for anything. But he said he had too much STUDYING to do.

I thought he was joking at first. I mean, the word NO isn't really in Sam's vocabulary. And I don't think I saw him crack open a book at all last year—not even once. But when I asked again, he got all wiggly.

"I can't," he said. "Sorry." Then he bounced away. SHEESH.

So I headed off to the library by myself. But when I got there, the door was locked. The lights were off.

That room was NOT open for business. And judging from the disgusting cobwebs stuck across the corner of the door, no one had been in there for weeks.

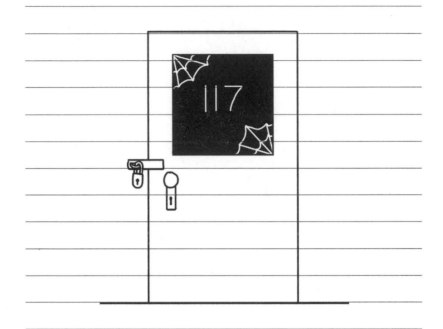

That's when Bones and his gang walked by. Bones is a spider jockey with a big mouth. So he's like, "Need some help there, Itchy?" He calls me that because he KNOWS it bugs me. In fact, just hearing it made me want to scratch my itchy skin—especially when I got some cobweb stuck to my face.

Anyway, I told Bones I had a meeting in the library, thank you very much. Then he pointed his bony finger and said, "Wrong room, GENIUS."

Sure enough, I was at the wrong door. See, the library is in Room 119. I was trying to bust down the door to Room 117. GREAT.

I crept next door to the library and found Mrs. Collins leading the meeting. She's our librarian, and also my Language Arts teacher. She whipped off her reading glasses as if she couldn't believe what she was seeing. "Gerald Creeper?" she said. "What a nice surprise."

Well, I was surprised too—let me tell you. Because there were only TWO other kids at that meeting. One was Whisper Witch, who pretty much signs up for every activity under the moon. The other was Emma Enderman. She's a sixth grader—new to school this year. But the girl acts like she owns the place. She's so tough, no one dares look her in the eye.

To top things off, Mr. ZANE was at the meeting. Now there's a zombie who knows how to suck the fun out of things. When he took over the talent show last year, I almost had to quit.

Did I mention the fact that Mr. Zane REEKED of something disgusting? Well, his briefcase did anyway. I could almost SEE the stench lines curling up toward my creeper nostrils. GREAT.

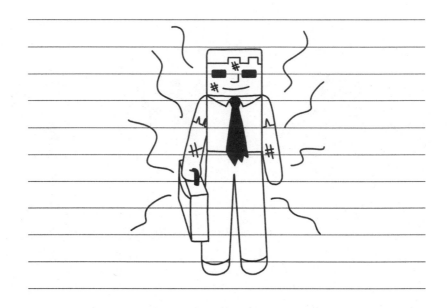

The smell was so bad, I missed half of what Mrs. Collins was saying—until she gave me my story assignment. I heard THAT loud and clear. "You can attend the Dance Committee tomorrow morning," she said. "Get the scoop on decorations, music, and so on. Won't that be fun?"

Um, NO. I couldn't make that story sound fun no matter how I looked at it—upside down, sideways, or straight on.

Then it hit me—dances have music. And RAP is a kind of music. I suddenly got an idea that was so GENIUS, I had to say it out loud. "Can I write a RAP about the school dance?" Maybe it would get printed in the paper. Maybe I could perform it over the loudspeaker. Maybe I could even perform it at the school dance!

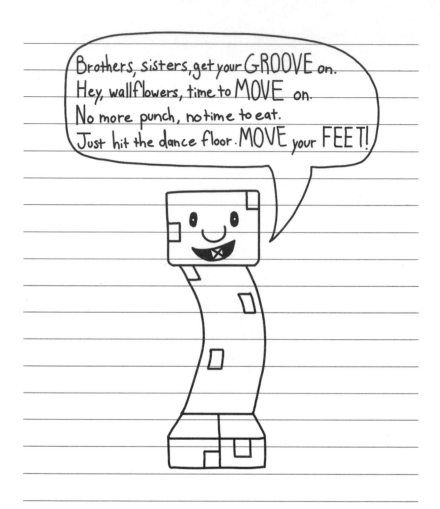

Mrs. Collins looked like she'd just swallowed a
spider's eye. Or maybe she'd finally gotten a whiff
of Mr. Zane's briefcase. She whispered something
to him, and then they both responded at the exact
same time.

RUDE! Teachers around _here_ don't really appreciate _my_ rap skills—even though I'm practically friends with Kid Z, the most famous rapper in the Overworld. I _thought_ about mentioning that to Mrs. Collins, but sometimes a creeper just has to cut his losses and move on.

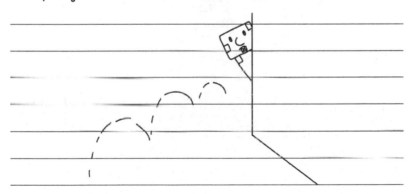

So Wednesday after school, I crept off toward that Dance Committee meeting. Well, first I looked for Sam, hoping I could drag him with me. But SOMEHOW, he had disappeared again!

I figured he was with his girlfriend, Willow Witch. They're ALWAYS together, even though she's two years older than him. I don't even want to THINK about how Sam will be when she starts tenth grade at Mob High School next year.

But he wasn't with Willow. How do I know, you ask? Because Willow was at the Dance Committee meeting. When I asked if she'd seen Sam, she looked at me all strange-like.

"I thought he was with you," she said. Turns out, Sam told Willow he couldn't go to the dance meeting because he was hanging out with ME.

I tried to cover for the slime, I really did. But it was too late. Willow could see I didn't have a clue where Sam was. I might have even mentioned that he'd been sneaking off a LOT lately.

Willow swore she'd hunt him down later and get to the bottom of it. I believed her, because that witch knows how to brew Potions of Invisibility. If she wants to find out where Sam's been going, she WILL.

I went home to try to sleep, but how's a creeper supposed to get his sleepers when his best friend is lying to him? And about to be busted by his angry girlfriend?

Anyway, you can imagine my surprise when I ran into Sam and Willow walking to school together that night. It didn't look like Sam was in trouble. Nope. He and Willow were all chummy, same as usual.

I tried to get Willow's attention to ask her what was up. I gave her all kinds of signs. I coughed, cleared my throat, blinked three times—the usual stuff.

But she pretty much ignored me. So I finally asked SAM where he'd been that morning. And you know what he said? He pulled the old "I've been STUDYING" line.

I waited for Willow to bust him, but she just fake-smiled. Which meant she knew where he'd ACTUALLY been. But neither one of them was going to tell me. Sam, who is usually an open book and can't keep a secret to save his life, had locked himself up like my sister Chloe's diary—and swallowed the key.

GULP

Sam acted _pretty_ normal on Thursday morning. But on Friday, when I asked if he wanted to hang out, he tried to pull his disappearing act again. So I followed him. I tracked him all the way to the library. Well, I stopped at Room 117 for like a SECOND to check the handle. Yup, still locked.

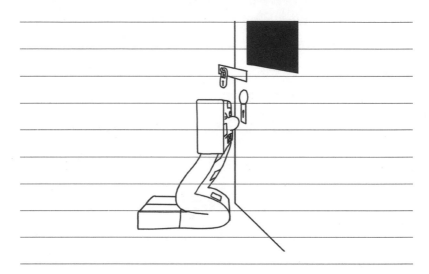

But by the time I got to the library, Sam was nowhere in sight. How does a giant bouncing slime slip away from a sneaky creeper? SHEESH.

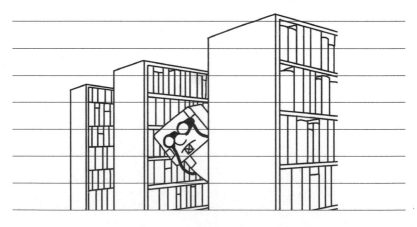

Mrs. Collins was at the checkout desk. When she asked how my article on the dance was coming, I said it was going GREAT—it was gonna be a real page turner, for sure. That's when I saw a familiar book on the desk. It was that Sherlock Bones book with a wolf on the cover—the one Mom had tried to get me to read. WOLF OF THE BLASTERVILLES, it was called.

When I picked it up, Mrs. Collins sprang out of her seat like a firework rocket.

"What a WONDERFUL book for you, Gerald!" she said. "Sherlock Bones is a detective, which is kind of like being a newspaper reporter, don't you think?"

Say WHAT? At first, I thought Mrs. Collins and Mom were in cahoots. Like, maybe she was working for Mom on the sly to get me to read more. (And I really don't appreciate it when adults gang up on kids like that.)

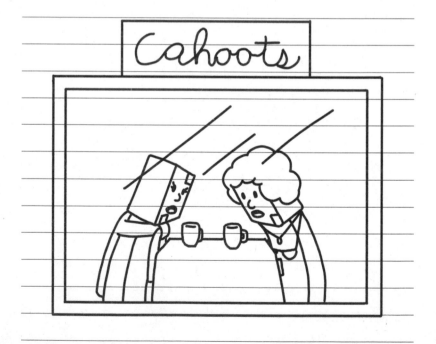

But then I thought about what Mrs. Collins had said. I guess newspaper reporters ARE kind of like detectives.

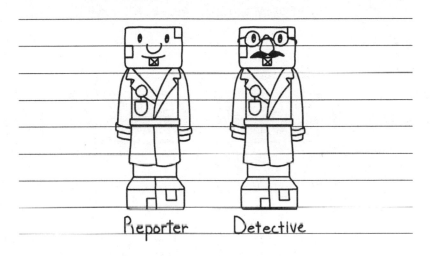

Reporter   Detective

I checked out the book, since Mrs. Collins was practically shoving it in my backpack. And as I left the library, I thought about some of the things I could "investigate" at school—besides the dance, I mean. Like, what's the mystery meat they serve in the cafeteria? And what REALLY goes on in the teachers' lounge?

The more I thought about it, the more excited I got. There were all KINDS of mysteries to solve. Maybe this newspaper thing could work out after all!

So I've decided to take Mom up on that 30-day plan.
I'll stick it out on the newspaper staff, reporting
on things kids REALLY want to know. Meanwhile, I'm
going to solve a few mysteries of my own:

30-Day Plan for Getting
to the Bottom of Things

• Find out why Room 117 is
ALWAYS locked.

• Discover what stinky thing
lives in Mr. Zane's briefcase.

• Figure out what in the
Overworld is going on with Sam.

That last one's the biggie. But I'm not going to
sweat it. Because I, Gerald Creeper Jr., am going
undercover. I'm going to find out what's REALLY
going on here at Mob Middle School.

DAY 2: SUNDAY

So I started reading THE WOLF OF THE
BLASTERVILLES, and I gotta say, this Sherlock Bones
dude is alright—I mean, for a skeleton and all. And
his spider sidekick, Dr. Webson, isn't half bad either.

I've already gotten TONS of tips for sleuthing. Like, I figured out right away that I needed a disguise. And I knew just where to get one.

My older sister Cate is pretty much the Fashion Queen. She's got a closet that's bigger than my room, I swear, and it's full of skins. She can walk in there looking like a creeper, and walk out looking like a zombie pigwoman. Or even a red-headed human.

Lately, Cate's been sporting what she calls the "au naturel" look, which I guess means straight-up creeper green. That's fine by me. It means there's more left over in her closet for ME to poke through.

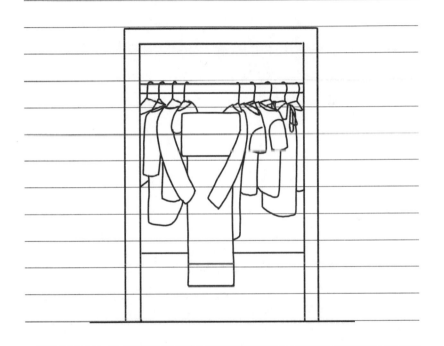

So after getting lost in there for a while (and I'm not even kidding), I walked out wearing a trench coat and cap, holding a magnifying glass. (Cate told me she uses the magnifying glass to pluck her eyebrows, but I'm going to pretend I didn't hear that.)

Cate said I looked "mysterious," which is pretty much what I was going for. But when I walked into the living room and held the magnifying glass up to my eye, my Evil Twin fell all over herself laughing. I guess my eye looked HUGE or something.

Then my baby sister Cammy started laughing too—so hard that she blew herself up (which is why we call her the Exploding Baby). That brought Mom running out of the kitchen, where she'd been trying to write her bestseller. UH-OH.

"How is an author supposed to get any work done around here?" she hollered.

I decided that was a good time to practice my sneaking-off skills, but I'm not nearly as good at that as Dad is. (He'd already disappeared.) If I was going to go undercover at school, I REALLY had to learn how to "pull a Dad."

POOF!

I found him hiding in the garage, which was the perfect place to hang out for a while. And he agreed to teach me everything he knows about creeping. We started with what he calls the art of DISTRACTION.

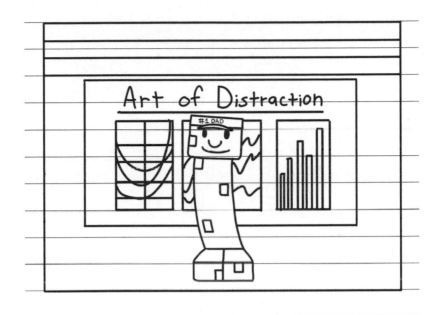

"Hey, Gerald," he said. "Have you seen my pickaxe lately?"

"Sure," I said. "It's hanging right over there." I showed him, but when I turned back around, Dad was gone.

"Gotcha!" he hollered, jumping out from behind the furnace. It was a TOTAL Dad move, but it was still kind of impressive.

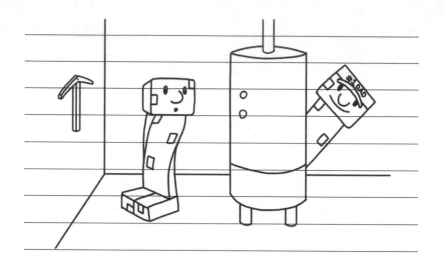

He did it again a few minutes later. "Could you get me some gunpowder out of that barrel?"

Yup, I fell for it again.

POOF!

Gunpowder

And again.

And AGAIN. How embarrassing!!!

But then it occurred to me that maybe someone

ELSE had been pulling this distraction trick on me—SAM. That slime had learned how to creep off with the best of them. But where was he going?

I've been thinking about it all night. I mean, I'm supposed to be writing my article about the dance. It's due Tuesday morning (YIKES!). But how can I write about streamers, jukeboxes, and disco balls when I'm worried about my best friend?

I've got what Mom would call a serious case of writer's block.

And it's shaped like a sneaky green slime.

DAY 4: TUESDAY

Where's Sherlock Bones when you need him?!

Let's just say that my first night as an undercover detective at Mob Middle School didn't go according to plan.

Everything started out okay. Right away in first period, Sam said he liked my cap. He didn't even question why I was wearing a cap and trench coat to science class. See, that's the way Sam is—he's not really an "ask a lot of questions" kind of guy. But I sure had some questions for him.

Except every time I tried to pin him down about where he went after school last Wednesday and Friday, he dodged my attacks. He pretended to be all interested in the fossils at the back of the room. He even asked if he could borrow my magnifying glass to examine them.

I tried to sound like an official detective. "Sam," I said, "based on the evidence, I'm DEDUCING that you have a secret."

He gave me his blank face and asked what "deducing" meant.

So I tried again. I said, "Sam, the facts just aren't adding up."

Deductions

$$4 + 8 \times 10 \div 3 \times 6$$
$$-7 + 26 \times 4 \times 7 +$$
$$13 \div 2 + 17 \times 5 \div$$
$$11 \div 3 - 6 \times 8 + 5$$
$$\times 19 + 21 \div 3 \times 6$$
$$+ 8 \div 3 \times 9 + 7 - 1$$
$$\times 5 \div 14 + 6 \times 3 = ?$$

He thought I was talking about math homework. SHEESH.

I tried again at lunchtime, but Sam invited Willow Witch to sit with us. I thought that was a pretty good opportunity to get my newspaper article written, since Willow is on the Dance Committee and all. But I still hadn't found my angle yet. I mean, what do mobs REALLY want to know about the dance?

Then I remembered. Last fall, everyone had gone CRAZY over the punch at the dance. I had a theory that there was a potion brewing in there—like a love potion or something. I'd even told Sam that Willow MUST have used a potion on him. I mean, why else would he be with her? But he hadn't really appreciated that deduction.

Anyway, I decided to ask Willow about it. I said, "My sources tell me there was something up

with the punch served at the dance last year.
An unnamed bystander said he MIGHT have seen
a fermented spider eye floating in the bowl.
Anything you want to tell me about that, Willow?
Anything at all?" I held up my magnifying glass and
stared at her. HARD.

She just snorted. "You're so weird, Gerald. Who do
you think you are, anyway? Sherlock Bones?"

YES! I took that as a compliment. It meant I was doing SOMETHING right. So I told her that I was, in fact, a student of Private Investigator Bones.

That's when Ziggy Zombie plunked down next to me. I swear, no matter how hard I try to put some distance between me and that zombie at lunchtime, I always end up sitting close enough to hear him smacking on his rotten flesh sandwiches.

"I LOVE Sherlock Bones!" he said. (SMACK, SMUCK, SQUISH) "Do you want to borrow my pet spider? He could be your Dr. Webson!"

Well, I'd met Ziggy's pet spider, Leggy. And that furry-legged critter was NO Dr. Webson, let me tell you. Besides, if I were going to hire a sidekick, it would have to be my pet squid, Sticky.

So I told Ziggy that although I appreciated his generous offer, I wouldn't be taking him up on it. No, I wouldn't need any help from that zombie at all, thank you very much.

Let's just say that I did NOT get my newspaper article written at lunch. Instead, I scratched something out after school. But I only had like 10 minutes! I didn't get very far before Mr. Zane staggered up and said I'd better not be late to the meeting.

I actually SMELLED Mr. Zane before I saw him. And as I followed the stench of his briefcase toward the library, I kind of wished I'd taken Ziggy up on his offer to help with my sleuthing.

See, Ziggy is the one mob that could probably help me identify the smell coming from Mr. Zane's briefcase. Why? Because it smelled an awful lot like what Ziggy ate for lunch.

As soon I walked into the library, Mrs. Collins
started collecting our articles. Luckily, Emma wanted
Mrs. Collins to read hers FIRST. She gave me the
evil Enderman eye, as if she thought I was going to
try to butt in line. She almost looked disappointed
that I didn't try.

Instead, I thought fast and scrawled a headline
across the top of my page: WHAT'S BREWING IN THE
PUNCH BOWL?

When I handed it to Mrs. Collins, she skimmed it quickly—all two paragraphs of it. Then she said, "Gerald, I think we might need to do a little FACT-checking on this article." I didn't exactly love her tone of voice.

Whisper Witch leaned over and offered to help me with research next time. "Nah, I got this," I told her. I kind of wished she would just keep her warty nose out of my business.

I decided I was going to dive into the next story and make it the BEST article the MOB MIDDLE SCHOOL OBSERVER had ever published. I was going to blow Mrs. Collins's socks right off—along with those little glasses she wears on a chain around her neck. Yup, I was going to out-sleuth even Sherlock Bones himself.

But that was all before I heard my next assignment. When Mrs. Collins gave it to me, my hopes and dreams fizzled like a wet firework.

"Gerald will interview the cafeteria staff about their plans to get more VEGETABLES into school lunches," Mrs. Collins announced.

GREAT. Beetroot soup, anyone?

I was almost ready to hang up my trench coat right
then and there—until I remembered my plan to unveil
the "mystery meat" that the cafeteria tries to pass
off as pork chops. Vegetables SMETCH-tables. I had a
WAY better story in mind.

When I caught a whiff of Mr. Zane's briefcase, I had
to stop thinking about food (or I was going to lose
my lunch right in the middle of the library). Before
I started investigating any mystery meat, I HAD to
figure out what was in that briefcase!

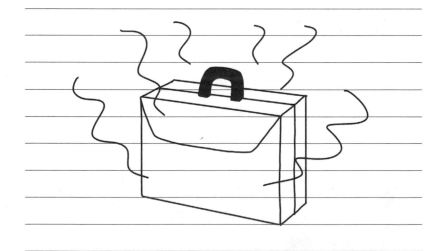

So after the newspaper meeting, I stuck around. I pretended to be super interested in the books in the back corner, right next to Mr. Zane's briefcase. And when he got up to talk to Mrs. Collins, I seized my opportunity. I dropped to the floor, grabbed that case, and flung it open to find the most AMAZING thing . . .

Well, that's what would have happened in a Sherlock Bones book maybe. But in the Gerald Creeper Jr. detective novels, things don't always go according to plan.

See, the briefcase was LOCKED. Locked up tight just like Room 117. So all I really did was knock the briefcase over. Which made a super loud BANG. Which meant EVERY mob in the library looked my way.

As Mr. Zane staggered toward me, I jumped up and grabbed a book off the shelf. "Found it!" I said, jogging toward the checkout desk.

Except I didn't exactly look at the cover of the book until I slapped it down on the desk. CHANGING

BODIES: A BOOK ABOUT THE FACTS OF LIFE the title
screamed in pink and blue letters.

GREAT.

I'm telling you, that would have NEVER happened
to Sherlock Bones. I REALLY have to step up my
sleuthing skills.

But right now? All I want to do is crawl into bed and pull the covers over my head. Maybe after a good day's sleep, I can forget the look on Mrs. Collins's face when she saw that library book. And everything I saw when I opened it up.

Wish me luck.

DAY 5: WEDNESDAY

Well, I didn't sleep a wink yesterday. I read a whole book instead. No, not THAT book. I mean, I might have peeked at the pictures in that one. And if any mobs want to know how their bodies are going to change over the next few years, I now have all the facts. WAY more than any creep ever needs to know.

The book I actually FINISHED reading was the Sherlock Bones mystery. That is NOT a short book, let me tell you. But the story sucked me right in.

(If Mom can write a mystery like that, we're gonna get rich for sure.)

See, in the book, this creeper family called the Blastervilles think they've been cursed by a legendary wolf—a wolf that FOLLOWS Henry Blasterville everywhere he goes. But it turns out the wolf is just a regular dog. Some bad dude got the dog to follow Henry by giving the dog one of Henry's boots to smell.

Well, that got me thinking. I could sure use a dog to follow SAM around—to find out where he's been sneaking off to. I don't have a dog, but I know someone who does: Eddy Enderman. He's got this wolf named Pearl. He loaned her to me once to pull a minecart through the snow. (But that's a whole other story.)

Anyway, I finally had a plan that could actually WORK. I decided that when I got to school last night, I was going to go see a boy about a wolf.

Eddy is pretty much the coolest kid at school, and we're sort of friends. But Eddy isn't exactly the kind of mob you can go up to and start a conversation with. No, you pretty much have to wait for HIM to come to YOU.

So I was sitting at lunch sketching a picture of a wolf on the back of a napkin. That was when Bones and his gang walked by. He leaned over my shoulder and and whispered in my ear.

Well, his skeleton buddies started laughing their bony butts off. But then Fate stepped in—in the form of an Enderman. Yup, Eddy showed up from out of nowhere, just when I needed _him_ most. (He's really good at that.)

He said really loud-like (to drown out Bones and his gang), "I hear you joined the newspaper staff. Very cool, dude."

That gave me the perfect chance to ask my burning question. It was like Eddy had opened up a portal for me to walk right through. I took a deep breath and asked if I could borrow his wolf for some "official newspaper business."

He shrugged and said sure. "When?"

"Um, Friday after school?"

"Cool. Later, Gerald."

Just like that. It was actually one of the longest conversations I'd had with Eddy—long enough for everyone in the cafeteria to look my way. I pretty much owe ALL my popularity to Eddy. When I'm a famous rapper, I'll have to mention him in an awards speech or something.

To Eddy Enderman. Very cool, dude.

But when I got home from school this morning, I realized something. If I want Eddy's wolf to help track Sam, she's going to need something of Sam's to sniff—something that has his smell on it. The dude doesn't have a very big wardrobe. So at first, I started to panic.

But now I'm staring at the PERFECT thing—one of Sam's T-shirts with a picture of his cat on it. Sam loaned it to me like a month ago, hoping I'd wear it. (He has this dream that me and Moo are going to be besties, but THAT's never going to happen. Did I mention I'm not a big fan of cats?)

I'm pretty sure the T-shirt still has Sam's smell on it. (At least there are little green blobs of slime here and there.) So I'll bring the shirt to school with me, and then we'll let Pearl the Wolf do her thing. We're going to track down Sam—and FINALLY crack the Case of the Sneaky Slime!

DAY 7: FRIDAY

You know, I gotta say, THE WOLF OF THE BLASTERVILLES was a great book. But the WOLF OF GERALD CREEPER JR? Not so much. If Mrs. Collins recommended that book to me, I'd probably march right back in and demand a refund—or at least an apology.

Seriously. Here's how it all went down: Eddy must have teleported home and back in a flash, because he met me in front of the school with Pearl like five minutes after the bell rang. She growled at me, of course. It's like the wolf has totally forgotten all the skeleton bones I fed her when we did our little sledding thing last winter.

Anyway, Pearl didn't have to like ME. She just had to smell SAM. So I got down to business. I pulled the T-shirt out of my backpack and gave her a good whiff.

Track, Pearl. Track!

She sat on her rump and stared at me like I was nuts. Then Eddy reminded me I had to bribe her with a bone—which I'd totally forgotten to bring. When Bones and his buddies walked by, I thought about asking him for a loaner. But Eddy handed me one instead.

I gave Pearl a few licks, and then I showed her Sam's shirt again. "Where's Sam, Pearl?" I said. "Go get 'im!"

And you know what? She took off! She tore up the steps to the school, straight through the doors, and past a bunch of surprised mobs in the hall.

I tried to keep up, but my short creeper legs don't move all that fast. I saw Pearl's silver tail disappear down the hall toward the library, so I ran that way too. Then I heard Pearl howling.

I THOUGHT she had found Sam. But she'd found someone else instead.

MR. ZANE. Yup, she'd tackled him right to the ground in the hallway. That poor zombie was sprawled out on the floor, and Pearl was biting at his briefcase like it was the most delicious bone she'd ever sunk her teeth into.

Eddy suddenly teleported into the hall and pulled Pearl off, but somehow, she'd already gotten that locked briefcase open. And you know what spilled out? The STINKIEST, SLIMIEST, MOLDIEST pile of rotten flesh I've ever seen—or smelled. Even Eddy took one LONG step backward.

Mrs. Collins hurried out of the library with a horrified look on her face. "Mr. Zane," she said, "Is that your, um, LUNCH?"

He grunted and said it was actually for his DOG. He said he takes the scraps home from the cafeteria every morning.

Well, I was pretty interested to hear that. I mean, it kind of proved my suspicions about the mystery meat in the cafeteria. I'd be quoting Mr. Zane in my newspaper article, for sure.

But I hadn't figured out a single thing about SAM.

When I pulled out Sam's slimy T-shirt again, Eddy said he had to get going. Before I knew it, he and Pearl had teleported away. POOF! And so had my big plan for figuring out where Sam had gone.

GREAT.

I mean, I guess I DID solve the Case of the Stinky Briefcase. (Mom always says I should focus on the positives.)

> ## 30-Day Plan for Getting to the Bottom of Things
>
> • Find out why Room 117 is ALWAYS locked.
>
> • ~~Discover what stinky thing lives in Mr. Zane's briefcase.~~
>
> • Figure out what in the Overworld is going on with Sam.

But how am I going to solve the other two mysteries? I'm fresh out of ideas. And I've already read my Sherlock Bones book cover to cover. Where am I supposed to get inspiration NOW?

DAY 8: SATURDAY

So I thought I'd been super sly at school. I thought I'd done a PRETTY good job of keeping my investigations undercover. But tonight after dinner, Chloe cornered me and made some crack about my "attack dog" tackling Mr. Zane. How'd she know about that???

Here's the thing: Chloe is the LAST creeper I want sniffing around my business. She's the MASTER at twisting the facts to make me look like the bad guy. (What can I say? She's had a whole lifetime of practice.)

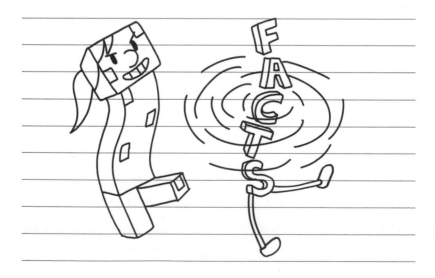

She kept asking me why I'd had Eddy's dog follow Mr. Zane. "What's so interesting about that zombie?" she said.

For some reason that I STILL don't know, I started to tell Chloe EVERYTHING. Maybe it was because I don't have a sidekick. I don't have a Dr. Webson, and it's really hard to figure out all this stuff on my own. So even though Chloe is at the BOTTOM of my list of possible sidekicks, I spilled.

I told her about Sam—that he's been sneaking around and giving me some line about "studying." Chloe kind of snorted when I said that. I guess EVERY mob knows that studying isn't really Sam's thing.

Well, it felt pretty good to get that off my chest, so I told Chloe about the mystery meat in the cafeteria. And about the rotten flesh in Mr. Zane's briefcase. And about Room 117.

Chloe actually looked kind of interested in that. Her eyes got all wide, and she leaned toward me. I thought she was going to help me make a plan for getting to the bottom of Room 117—or at least through the locked door.

But she didn't. You know what she said? She said there were some strange things going on in our VERY OWN HOUSE.

She led me to the back of her closet. "Listen," she whispered, putting her ear to the wall.

So I did. And I _heard this weird tapping sound_—like
a tiny creeper trying to axe his way out. There was
SOMETHING in the wall, that's for sure.

I freaked out and asked Chloe if it was silverfish,
because I'm REALLY not a fan of silverfish. But

she reminded me that silverfish make more of a SCRATCHING and SQUEAKING sound. (GROSS.)

Anyway, I decided that it was time to use my genius brain to figure this tapping thing out. See, Chloe's room backs up to Mom and Dad's room. There's a strict Creeper Family rule that we kids stay out of their room. But Dad was working on a minecart in the garage, and Mom must have been writing in her new backyard office (a.k.a., the chicken coop).

So we snuck into their room and examined every INCH of it. No silverfish. No endermites. No little creepers with pickaxes.

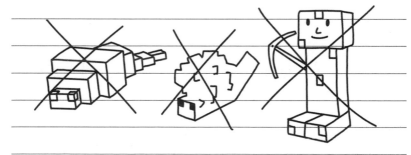

"So what's making the noise?" Chloe asked. She looked like a wolf, hot on the trail of a suspect's scent. She REALLY wanted to figure this thing out.

But I told her I couldn't really help her anymore right now, because I have a couple of my OWN mysteries to solve first. Oh, and another newspaper article to write. I did make a suggestion though: I told Chloe she should check out some of Mom's Agatha Crispy novels. Maybe Agatha Crispy will inspire Chloe the way Sherlock Bones inspired ME.

DAY 9: SUNDAY

So Mom's on Day 9 of writing her bestseller, but she says she's still working on chapter one. Now I'm no famous author, but I'm thinking she'd better get a move on—PRONTO. And I made the mistake of telling her that.

Being a detective and all, I probably should have noticed Mom's bloodshot eyes and the coffee stain on her sweater. I should have DEDUCED that it wasn't exactly the best time to offer her suggestions.

She almost blew her top, but she didn't. She just said in a flat voice that she'd probably be DONE with her book if she could get some peace and quiet around here.

I started to argue, but Dad crept past and shot me a warning look. So I decided to let Mom's comment go. Then I tried a new approach: I offered to HELP Mom with her project, the same way Whisper Witch offered to help me research my newspaper article.

That was when I remembered I still had an article to write—due in TWO days. I probably should have been working on my own stuff instead of helping Mom write her bestseller.

But Mom said she didn't need my help. And that no one was going to read a single PAGE of her book until it was finished. She actually stepped in front of her laptop, guarding it like an iron golem—as if her book held all kinds of secrets or something.

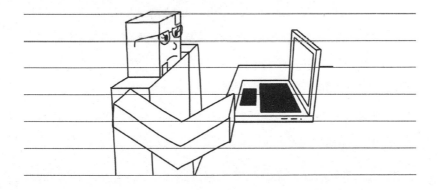

Mom suddenly reminded me of someone else I knew—Sam. Was that HIS big secret too? Was he writing a bestselling novel on the sly?

I almost laughed out loud. I've heard Sam try to write rap songs, so I KNOW he's no writer.

I have a cat
Her name is Moo.
Um... one plus one
equals TWO!

I'm not sure Mom is either, but she was sure giving it her best shot. When Dad offered to take my sisters to the Mob Mall so she could have some peace and quiet, Mom actually smiled at him. I know how much Dad HATES the mall, so I had to admit— that was a pretty generous offer.

After they left, Mom said she was heading to her office in the backyard. "Don't disturb me till breakfast time," she said.

No problem there. The LAST place you'll find me around here is in the chicken coop. (I'm not a big fan of those birds.)

So while Mom writes out back, I've been trying to write my newspaper article. But I haven't exactly interviewed the cafeteria staff about the mystery meat yet. I mean, Mr. Zane gave me some pretty good clues with his stinky briefcase. But Mrs. Collins said she wanted me to get ALL the facts this time.

So I've decided that tomorrow at lunchtime, I'll get the facts. I'll march right into that cafeteria kitchen and get to the bottom of that meat.

But right now? I think I'll just march into our own kitchen and get myself a snack. Brain food, I call it. All this detective work kind of makes a creep HUNGRY.

I'm hungry!

DAY 11: TUESDAY

So last night instead of sitting with my friends at lunch, I slipped into the cafeteria kitchen to investigate the mystery meat.

Lunchtime isn't exactly the BEST time to interview staff in the cafeteria. I mean, it was pretty noisy back there, with bowls of mushroom stew slopping their way down the lunch line and pork chops flinging off the grill.

On the other hand, it was the PERFECT time to examine a pork chop. I snuck one out of the warming bin when no one was looking. But when I pulled out my magnifying glass, this witch with a hairnet asked me what I thought I was doing.

I read her nametag and said politely, "Ms. Wilma, my eyes tell me that this is no ORDINARY pork chop. What's in this thing, anyway? Chicken? Fish? Moldy mushrooms? My nose detects a hint of rotten flesh . . ."

Ms. Wilma wasn't loving my sleuthing skills, I could tell. She pointed a crooked finger toward the back of the line and said that if I wanted a rotten-flesh chop, I could wait in line for it, just like every other kid. Then she snatched the chop away.

Well, that was all the RESEARCH I needed to do. Ms. Wilma had pretty much admitted she was serving up rotten-flesh chops, right?

So I went back to the lunch table and started working on my article. The headline practically wrote itself: "MYSTERY MEAT: A MYSTERY NO MORE!" I even drew a picture of a rotten-flesh chop with wiggly stench lines above it.

So everything was going my way. I had cracked the Case of the Stinky Briefcase, AND the Case of the Mystery Meat.

But you know what happened this morning after school? Mrs. Collins shot down my article. Yup, she handed it right back to me and said that I was writing FICTION, not facts.

Emma Enderman got this smug smile and said that
newspaper reporting was clearly "not my thing." But
Mrs. Collins said she was willing to give me another
chance. She said maybe I could choose my own topic
this time, as long as I did LOTS of research.

After the meeting, Whisper Witch followed me out.
She asked me again if I wanted any help. But I think

I'm starting to get how Mom feels about her novel. I mean, maybe I haven't solved a big mystery or written an award-winning article YET. But I still have 19 days. So if everyone would just back off, I'll figure this thing out.

Now I'm sitting at home, staring out my bedroom window. Mom sometimes says that "when one portal closes, another one opens." (She has all kinds of sayings like that.) I think it means that if something doesn't go your way, you should try something else. At least that's what she says when her 30-day plans don't work out.

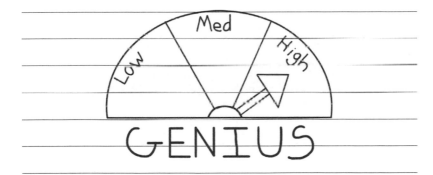

Anyway, I JUST had a genius idea. (What can I say? They hit me sometimes. . . . I'm wondering if Mom's saying works for LOCKED doors too. Because Room 117 has a door that's always locked—a door that's so full of cobwebs, no one ever gets through. But Room 117 probably ALSO has a window.

And if I get to school early tonight, I can check it out—look through that window and try to see what in the Overworld is going on in that room.

Who knows? Maybe that portal will even OPEN . . .

DAY 12: WEDNESDAY

Well, I got to school so fast last night, I practically teleported. I found the library window and then crept to the one next to it—the window to Room 117.

It was dark inside. No surprise there. I ALMOST walked away, but that's when I saw it—the glow of a TORCH. Coming from inside the room. Someone was in there!

But how'd they get in? The window was locked up tight—I examined every edge of it, wondering if someone had crawled through. Then I remembered my magnifying glass. See, Sherlock Bones would already be on his hands and knees looking for footprints. So I dropped down too. And guess what? I found some!

The footprints were about yea big and wide. Square, like the shape of my feet. About the SIZE of my feet, too, which I thought was a real coincidence. Until it hit me.

They WERE my footprints.

Yup, those are the moments in a detective's life when he's GLAD he doesn't have a sidekick—that there's no one there to witness his mortification. Except . . . lucky me! There WAS a witness after all. Someone cleared her throat—and asked me what I was doing face-down on the ground.

I glanced up and saw Mrs. Enderwoman's long black legs. She's my friend Eddy's mom, and also my history teacher. As I stared at her legs, trying to avoid her eyes, I had to think FAST. I told her I was examining the "architecture" of the school building. I figured a history teacher would eat up that sort of thing. (I know—genius, right?)

Mrs. Enderwoman said there were plenty of books about building and architecture in the library, if I wanted to learn more. She went on and on about how the school rooms were designed for "very specific purposes" and that there might be a "floor plan" of the school in the library, too.

A WHAT now? I asked her to repeat that.

She said a floor plan was like a map of all the rooms—ALL the rooms. Well, that had to mean Room 117 too, right?

I swear my nose started itching, as if it could SMELL the clues I could get from a map like that. So when school started, I headed for the library. Mrs. Collins was happy to make me a copy of the map—ecstatic, in fact. (Especially after I said Mrs. Enderwoman had assigned me a project on architecture. I mean, it wasn't a TOTAL fib.)

Anyway, I stuffed the map in my locker before anyone could ask about it. But now I'm home, and I've studied every inch of that map. And I've already DEDUCED something important—something that might help me crack the case of Room 117.

See, Room 117 doesn't have just one door. It has TWO. One leads into the hall—that's the one that's always locked. No surprise there. But guess where the other one leads?

Into the LIBRARY.

So I might have just found a way into Room 117 after all.

DAY 13: THURSDAY

You know how I was celebrating the other day because I didn't have a sidekick—no one to see me examining my OWN footprint with a magnifying glass?

Well, here's the thing. It's nice not to have witnesses when you do something dumb. But it sure would be nice to have a sidekick when you figure out something BRILLIANT.

I could barely sleep yesterday because of that map—because I'd found a new door to Room 117. And I would have given ANYTHING for a Dr. Webson, someone I could share my secret with. I tried talking to Sticky, but he just floated around in his aquarium staring at me. He was more like Dr. WET-son than Dr. Webson.

I suddenly really, really, REALLY wanted to talk to Sam. I mean, that slime is the one I tell when bad things happen. And he's the one I tell when good things happen.

I decided that I HAD to tell him about Room 117. Maybe he could help me figure out what was going on in there. And maybe figuring out THAT mystery would somehow help me figure out what was going on with Sam, too.

So as soon as I got to school last night, I found Sam. I pulled him with me into the janitor's closet, grabbed that map out of my backpack, and spread it out on the floor by the mop buckets. Then I told Sam I'd been investigating Room 117.

"Wait, is that the room by the library?" he asked.

"That's the room you get to THROUGH the library," I
announced, happy to share my latest deduction.

That's when Sam got all weird. He started jiggling,
the way he does before a test or when he's hyped
up on hot chocolate. And suddenly, he wouldn't
look me in the eye. I might as well have been an
Enderman.

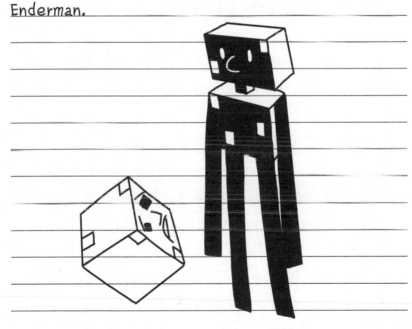

I asked Sam if he knew what was going on in Room 117. And I could TELL that he did. But he wouldn't say a word! When the bell rang, he mumbled something about science class and practically flattened me on his way out the door.

Well, after that whole closet scene, I couldn't WAIT to get to the library to look for the door to Room 117. If that's where Sam had been going all this time, I HAD to find out what was in there!

At lunchtime, I told Sam I had a stomachache—that I must have eaten a rotten potato for breakfast or something. I don't think he heard a word I said. He was still acting all weird and jittery. So while he wiggled off to find Willow, I snuck toward the library. I hoped I'd have it all to myself.

The bad news? Mr. Zane was in the library. The good news? He didn't have his briefcase with him. Maybe after the whole wolf attack, he'd decided to come up with a better place to store his stinky meat.

Anyway, when Mr. Zane asked if he could help me with anything, I told him I was just "browsing the books." I made SURE this time to avoid the Facts of Life section. Instead, I skimmed over the biographies. I slid past a few books about Redstone railways. And the whole time, I was creeping closer and closer to where I THOUGHT the door to Room 117 should be.

At first, I didn't see it. I crept down a whole row of bookshelves and back again. Nothing! Just shelf, shelf, shelf, painting, shelf, shelf . . .

Then I took a closer look. (I mean, I AM a detective, right?) And I spotted something. That painting of potted plants hanging on the wall WASN'T hanging on the wall. It was hanging on a DOOR!

I almost let out a "WHOOP," but I sure didn't need Mr. Zane staggering over. So I tried to play it cool. I found the doorknob behind the painting, and I very carefully gave it a turn. Well, I TRIED to, but the door was locked. (I know. Big surprise there, right?)

Now I'm not really the giving-up kind of creeper. So instead of creeping away, I took another look. I even pulled out my magnifying glass to look for clues—like fingerprints or cobwebs or ANYTHING.

There weren't any. But then I remembered something that I'd read in my Sherlock Bones book. See, sometimes what you DON'T see is actually a clue. If there weren't any cobwebs, then mobs were actually USING this door! At least ONE mob. Was it Sam?

When someone shuffled up behind me, I almost jumped out of my skin. Seriously—I nearly blew up right there in the library.

When I spun around, I must have still been holding up my magnifying glass, because Mr. Zane jumped too. (Did I mention how ginormous my eye looks through that thing?)

Anyway, when Mr. Zane asked what I was doing, I made up some excuse about how I was examining the painting—to be sure it wasn't a fake. "I'd hate to think that Mob Middle School was getting ripped off or something," I said.

Then I got out of there quick.

So now I'm home, and I've figured out a few things. Four things, actually:

- I'm getting pretty good at this detective thing. I mean, that line I fed Mr. Zane about the fake painting? That was genius. Just saying . . .

- Something sketchy is going on in Room 117. Why else would someone hide the doorway with a painting?

- Sam knows what's going on in Room 117. But he's not the smartest slime in the swamp, so he can't be the brains behind the operation. So . . . who is?

- That slime needs my help. He's probably in WAY over his head!!!

DAY 14: FRIDAY

What would Sherlock Bones do? That's the question I kept asking myself yesterday before I fell asleep. And I ended up having this dream that I WAS Sherlock Bones.

Yup, I looked down and I had these skeleton arms and bony skeleton fingers. And I was RIDING on a spider. It wasn't exactly Dr. Webson. It was Leggy, Ziggy's spider. (What can I say? Dreams are weird that way.)

Anyway, we were hot on the Case of the Potato
Thief. See, someone had been stealing crispy
potatoes out of the refrigerator. Now that might
not be a case Sherlock Bones would be interested
in, but I, Gerald Creeper Jr., have a thing for crispy
potatoes. If someone is stealing them, I want to
KNOW.

So I did what any good detective would do—I set a
trap. Well, actually, Leggy set a trap. He spun this
web right across the refrigerator door. Then we
waited around the corner.

It didn't take long before we heard a loud hiss, and when we got back into the kitchen, CHLOE was all wrapped up in that spider web. BUSTED. With a chunk of crispy potato on her cheek.

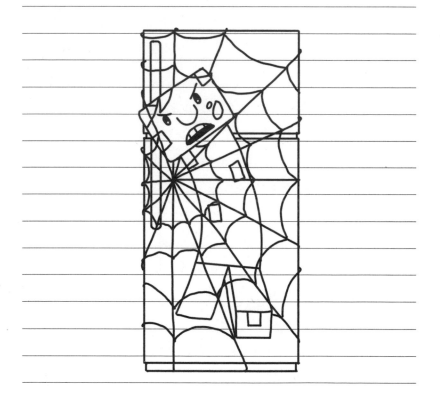

I woke up right away, because I HATE spider webs. (I once got caught in a ferocious cave spider's web, but that's a whole other story.) Anyway, I jumped in the shower to wash off the memory of my dream.

And suddenly, I had one of my genius ideas.

See, if I want to know who's been going in and out of Room 117, I have to do what Sherlock Bones would do. Or what Ziggy's pet spider, Leggy, would do. I have to set a TRAP.

All the way to school last night, I tried to psych myself up to join Web Weaving. Maybe I'd only have to take a class or two—just long enough to weave a web to stretch across the door of Room 117. But by the time I got to school, I had an even BETTER idea.

Remember how Ziggy was bugging me about helping with my investigations? Well, I said to myself, "Self, why do you want to learn how to weave a web when ZIGGY can do it for you?" Well, not actually Ziggy—but Ziggy's spider. (Most mobs don't know this about me, but I'm really all about teamwork.)

So I decided to talk to Ziggy about it at lunch. But you know what that zombie said? Well, I didn't hear EVERYTHING he said because there was a whole lot of smacking going on. But he said he was only JOKING about bringing Leggy to school. Because I guess there are rules about that sort of thing.

Anyway, his new idea was that we should hang out at HIS house and get Leggy to weave a cobweb THERE. Then we could snip the strings and bring it to school on Monday.

I gotta say, it wasn't a HORRIBLE idea. I mean, I don't love hanging out at Ziggy's house. The whole place kind of smells like Mr. Zane's briefcase, and I almost ALWAYS get stuck in one of Leggy's cobwebs. But here's the thing: it'll be a whole lot easier to sneak a cobweb into school than it would be to sneak a SPIDER into school. So I'm going over to Ziggy's tomorrow night.

As soon as I said yes, Ziggy got all weird and started talking like Sherlock Bones. As if HE were the detective and I was his sidekick. "Elementary, my dear Gerald. Elementary," he kept saying, with rotten-flesh juice dripping off his chin.

So, yeah. I'm pretty much already regretting my decision. All I can say is, this cobweb thing better pay off. BIG-TIME.

DAY 15: SATURDAY

Waiting for a spider to spin a web is like waiting for mushroom stew to boil. If you watch it and wait for it, it NEVER happens!

I thought I could go to Ziggy's, get the cobweb, and get out—keep the visit short and sweet, you know? But that's not what happened. While I followed Leggy around, waiting for him to spin a web, Ziggy followed ME around. "Gerald, you want to see my blister?" "Gerald, you want to hear my new 'Stagger and Stomp' playlist?" "Gerald, want to go freak out some villagers?"

He almost got me with that last one. See, Ziggy lives near a human village, and he's pretty good at sneaking up on villagers and spying on them. He likes to moan and groan just to freak them out. I guess it's Ziggy's hidden talent.

Anyway, I tried to stay focused—I had a case to solve, for cryin' out loud. So I told Ziggy that I had to stay close to Leggy. I waited and I watched. The WHOLE night.

I ate dinner with Ziggy (avoiding the rotten-flesh meatballs), ate lunch with Ziggy (avoiding the rotten-flesh tacos), and even ate BREAKFAST with Ziggy (avoiding the rotten-flesh sausages). I told his parents that I couldn't eat meat on Saturdays or Sundays—that it was a creeper thing.

I killed about as much time as a creeper can kill—but still, no cobwebs. Ziggy said he thought we were making Leggy nervous by staring at him. So I tried looking away. But every time I snuck a peek at Leggy, he was watching me, too. It was like a creeper-spider showdown.

Dawn was about to break, and I knew Mom and Dad would want me home. I also knew that Ziggy HAD to be in bed by dawn—his parents are pretty strict about that sort of thing. But I couldn't leave without a cobweb. I couldn't!

So when Ziggy asked me to sleep over, I said yes. While I called my parents, Ziggy put down this tattered old sleeping bag next to his bed. Well, I wasn't going to touch that stinky bag with a ten-foot pole—no sirree. Instead, I said I was going to get a glass of water. I figured that by the time I got back, Ziggy would be snoring up a storm. And I was right.

But someone else wasn't. See, Ziggy has this baby sister, Zoe, who isn't a big sleeper. The last time I stayed at Ziggy's, Zoe and I hung out during the day while the rest of the zombies got their Z's. I figured that if I hung with Zoe, I MIGHT catch Leggy spinning a web—and be able to get out of there before the sun went down.

Turns out, Zoe had ALL kinds of plans for me. We
had a tea party with her pet chicken. We sang
nursery rhymes (well, we RAPPED them).

Old McGerald had a farm, EE-I, EE-I, YO,
And on that farm he had a chicken, EE-I, EE-I, YO.
With a BAWK, BAWK here
And a BAWK, BAWK there,
Here a BAWK, there a BAWK,
Everywhere a BAWK BAWK..

We even played hide-and-seek. When it was my turn
to hide, I snuck under the kitchen table. BIG mistake.
There were chunks of rotten flesh EVERYWHERE. But
when I looked up, you know what I saw?

Leggy. In a freshly spun COBWEB.

Turns out Leggy was hiding under the table, too. Let me just tell you, I have NEVER been more excited to see a cobweb in my life.

I sprang into action. See, I brought something with me to capture that web. It took some genius planning ahead of time. I knew I'd need a way to bring that web home WITHOUT touching it. (My skin itches just thinking about touching that web.)

So I packed the biggest, best web catcher I could think of—the floor plan of Mob Middle School. It's perfect! It's big enough to fit the whole web, but I can roll it up small enough to stick in my backpack.

Leggy wasn't thrilled with my plan. He didn't exactly want to move out of the way and let me tear down his web. But then I got an idea. I happen to know that Leggy likes rotten flesh. (I guess when you're raised in a zombie house, you have to eat SOMETHING.)

So I used my foot to nudge some slimy flesh nuggets out from under the table. It wasn't easy, let me tell you. I wanted to hurl more than once. But I managed to make this whole trail of chunks leading toward the living room. And Leggy took the bait.

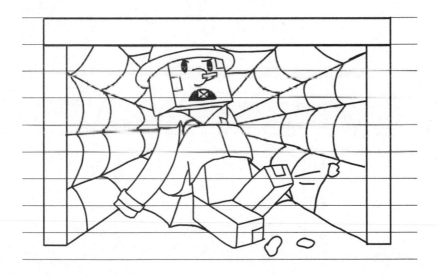

As soon as he was gone, I scooped up that web with my map. Then I rolled it up, carefully as I could, and started to sneak out of the house.

But Zoe busted me. "I found you!" she said. So I had to play a whole other round of hide-and-seek, pretending like I didn't see her hiding in the EXACT same spot under the table. A creeper's gotta do what a creeper's gotta do, right?

Anyway, I finally got out of there and back home.
And now it's time to figure out Phase 2 of my
master plan. I got the web out of Ziggy's house.
But how am I going to get it INTO the library? Man,
a detective's work is never done.

I'm gonna have to sleep on this one. There are
only a few hours of daylight left, and all that
spider-chasing at Ziggy's wore me out. Now if only I
could get Zoe's nursery rhymes out of my head . . .

DAY 16: SUNDAY

I can think of lots of GREAT ways to wake up, like
when . . .

- you jump out of bed, thinking it's time to go to
  school, but then you realize it's the weekend.
  Ahh . . .

- you wake up to moonlight streaming through your
  window.

- you wake up from the perfect dream, where you're a famous rapper taking a bow after a sold-out show . . .

But you know what's NOT a good way to wake up? With your sister Chloe staring at you, her green mug two inches away from your face. That's pretty much a daymare.

Anyway, she woke me up tonight because she was hearing things in her closet again. STRANGE things.

I pretty much slept-walked into her room. A creep can't do his best work on two hours of sleep. But I gotta say, when I got into Chloe's closet, I woke right up.

The tapping noise was louder now. And Chloe showed me a tiny crack in her wall—with a prick of light shining through. From WHAT? A torch? Lava? Fire?

That's when Chloe said she thinks her closet might back up to a PORTAL—the kind you can't see until you activate it. The kind that leads to the Nether. Or even to THE END. "And you know what you find if you go through the End Portal?" she said.

I did. Going through an End Portal means meeting up with the deadliest mob of all—the Ender Dragon. I started picturing that fierce dragon in my mind, and at that exact moment, I heard a loud scraping noise—like a giant dragon claw scratching against stone.

Well, I'm not gonna lie—I jumped so high, I nearly hit my head on Chloe's ceiling. I got OUT of that closet pronto.

Was Chloe scared too, or was she just trying to freak me out? I couldn't tell.

But now I'm back in my own room, and all I can think about is Room 117. Because after seeing what I saw in Chloe's closet, I'm starting to wonder. Is the doorway in the library MORE than just a door?

Could it maybe, possibly . . . be a portal too?

DAY 18: TUESDAY

You know, I knew Sam was in over his head. But after what happened last night at school, I'm starting to think I'M in trouble, too.

At first, everything went according to plan. I woke up early, grabbed my backpack (with the map and Leggy's cobweb inside), and headed off to school. Ziggy was going to meet me there.

I didn't love that idea at first. I'm kind of a loner when it comes to my detective work. But then I remembered how good Ziggy is at spying on villagers, and I started thinking he'd make a good lookout guy—you know, the one who watches for teachers or other mobs to creep up on us when we're planting our trap.

So I got to school and waited for Ziggy in the moonlight. Then we crept inside. There weren't any students there yet—just the zombie janitors. PERFECT, right?

The library was dark, and we decided to keep it that way. Ziggy planted himself in the doorway, and I crept toward the painting that hangs between the bookshelves. I was so nervous, I could hear my heart pounding in my ears. I swear, I could almost hear that creepy music that plays in movies, too—right before someone gets ATTACKED.

"Stay cool," I kept telling myself, imagining that Eddy Enderman was there. "Be cool, dude."

And I was. Until I got to the painting—the secret doorway to Room 117. Because here's the thing: The library was empty, but Room 117 WASN'T. Weird flashes of light spilled out around the edges of the door.

That's when I knew: Room 117 MUST be a portal. But a portal to WHERE?

When Ziggy groaned at me to hurry up, I kicked it up a notch. I unrolled the map, held it up to the doorway, and gave the edges a good press—just to make sure the cobweb stuck. But some of the web stuck to the map. And some of the web stuck to ME. (YUCK!)

There wasn't enough web left in the doorway to trap a mob—not a big one, anyway. And that web SURE wasn't going to trap a monster. I could picture the Ender Dragon tearing its way right through that web with its sharp claws. Easy-peasy.

Pretty much all a creeper could hope for was that there was enough cobweb left to give me a few clues. Like, if I came back later and saw the cobweb had been broken, I'd KNOW that a mob—or monster—passed through. And if I saw pieces of cobweb stuck on some mob's face or clothes, I'd know WHO had come through the door to Room 117.

So I zipped up my backpack and got out of the library before anyone could bust me and Ziggy. And the rest of the night?

Well, that was pure torture. The WAITING was killing me. And it didn't help when Ziggy almost let our whole plan slip out at lunchtime.

He was really yawny—like my sister Cammy gets when she needs a nap. When Willow asked him if he'd please stop yawning and keep his mouth closed while he chews, he said he couldn't help it. He said, "Me and Gerald got up early to—"

Well, he would have finished that sentence if I hadn't kicked him under the table.

A chunk of sandwich flew out of his mouth, and then he shut right up. "Sorry," he said to me.

But now it was out there. I had to think fast. "We got up early to . . . um, spy on villagers," I said.

"Without ME?" said Sam. He looked like he was going to start blubbering, which I thought was pretty rude considering HE was the one who had pretty much abandoned ME this semester. Didn't that slime know I was doing all of this top-secret stuff to try to help him?

Anyway, I couldn't worry about that because I had just spotted Mrs. Collins in the lunchroom, which meant I could finally sneak off to the library and check our

trap. I told Sam that I had to run to the restroom—
that the mystery meat from the cafeteria was messing
with me. But instead, I raced to the library.

I could barely breathe, let me tell you. Especially
when I lifted up that painting of the potted plants
and saw that . . . THE COBWEB WAS BROKEN. Someone
had come out that door! A mob who probably had a
face full of cobwebs by now. And all I had to do was
spot him or her. Gerald Creeper Jr. was on the case.

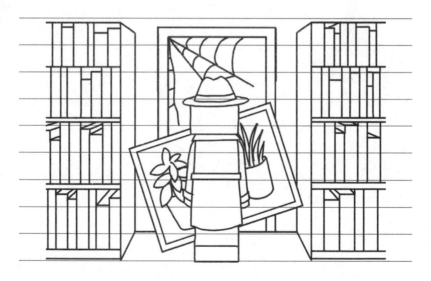

But I was so focused on spotting that cobweb that
I totally forgot something else: I had a newspaper

article to write—by the end of the school night. Which came MUCH faster than I thought it would.

I was sitting in the newspaper staff meeting wondering how I was going to get out of this mess. I mean, I wasn't exactly rocking the newspaper reporting thing. My first two articles had been a bust. And article three? I hadn't written a single word. I mean, I'd been kind of busy lately, you know?

But as I was wracking my genius brain, trying to come up with an excuse, I spotted something. Something white and sticky—dangling from Mrs. Collins's hair. A COBWEB.

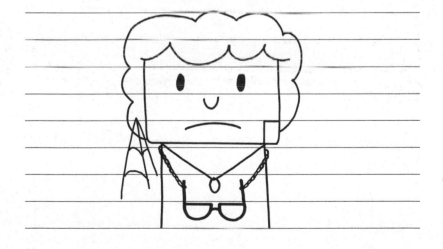

A gazillion thoughts exploded in my head. What was Mrs. Collins doing in Room 117? Had she passed through a portal? Had she taken Sam with her?

That was when she busted me. "Gerald," she said, "what are you staring at, dear?"

I *thought fast, like usual. I told Mrs. Collins that I*
was admiring her glasses. But I hadn't really thought
that one through, because next thing I knew, Mrs.
Collins was letting me borrow those glasses. And
telling me which shop at the Mob Mall sold them.
And the whole time I'm wearing those glasses with
the little chain around my neck, Emma Enderman was
busting a gut laughing at me.

NOT my best moment, let me tell you.

But I couldn't be worried about my reputation when I'd pretty much just cracked the case of Room 117. Or at least cracked it partway open.

When Mrs. Collins asked if I'd finished my article, I pushed her glasses up on my nose and told her that I had NOT. But that I was really close to getting it done. And that it was quite an important story—that I was SURE it would be worth her wait if she'd give me just a tiny extension.

Which she did. Which was kind of a miracle.

Then, as I followed Whisper Witch out the door, Mrs. Collins called me back. UH-OH. My heart started doing that THUD-THUD thing again. Did she KNOW I was on to her? I couldn't tell.

I tried to play it cool as she crept closer to me. And CLOSER. I nearly blew out of my creeper skin. What did she want from me???

"My glasses," she finally said.

OH. Phew.

Then she said I seemed kind of jumpy lately.
She said maybe I should STOP reading detective
novels—that Sherlock Bones was kind of making my

imagination run wild. She said I should try something different, like this book called FRANKEN-SLIME.

FRANKEN-
SLIME

Mary Shulker

"It's about a scientist who creates a monster slime in his science lab," she said. "No clues. No culprits. No magnifying glasses or mysteries."

"So no FUN?" is what I wanted to say. But I took the book. Now that I knew Mrs. Collins had something to do with Room 117, I wanted to get out of that library as fast as I could.

When I got home this morning, I propped the book up on my desk. It REALLY didn't look like my kind of book, but I thought Sticky might enjoy looking at the picture of Franken-Slime. (The squid's gotta get kind of bored in that aquarium, you know?)

Then I got to thinking . . . Maybe Mrs. Collins gave me that book for a reason. Maybe she's trying to send me a MESSAGE. Grown-ups do that kind of thing—especially SNEAKY grown-ups. And I'm starting

to see that Mrs. Collins isn't the sweet old creeper
she seems to be ...

So I've decided to start reading FRANKEN-SLIME. If
Mrs. Collins is trying to tell me something, I'm ALL
ears.

DAY 20: THURSDAY

Okay, if Mrs. Collins thought that reading FRANKEN-SLIME would make me LESS jumpy, she's had a few too many rotten potatoes or something. That book does NOT make for sweet dreams, let me tell you. I finished it this morning, and I didn't sleep a wink after that.

It's about this scientist named Victor Frankenslime
who works in a lab. He does all these experiments
and ends up creating something. What does he
create? (Drum roll here . . .) A SLIME!

Yup, he creates a slime like SAM. But it's not a REAL
slime. No, sirree. It's more like a MONSTER.

So if Mrs. Collins was trying to send me a message,
I've got it, loud and clear. There's only one thing I
can DEDUCE from all the clues I've uncovered. Let's
just recap them here, shall we?

Clues

- Sam has been acting strange.

- There's something strange going on in Room 117.

- Sam KNOWS what's going on in Room 117.

- Mrs. Collins has BEEN in Room 117.

- Mrs. Collins is a fan of FRANKEN-SLIME.

- FRANKEN-SLIME is a book about experiments done on a SLIME.

You don't have to be a genius to put it all together, right? I mean, it all adds up!

MRS. COLLINS HAS BEEN DOING EXPERIMENTS ON SAM!!!

Oh, man. This is WAY worse than I thought. Way, WAY worse.

But I am NOT going to leave my best friend hanging on this one. I'm going to figure out EXACTLY what Mrs. Collins has been doing to him, and I'm going to put a STOP to it. That librarian is messing with the WRONG slime!

DAY 21: FRIDAY

You know, I'm a creeper who doesn't like to ask for help. (I mean, except for when I had to bring in Ziggy to make that sticky trap.) But I got to thinking this Sam situation might be too big for me, you know? Like maybe I should talk to Mom and Dad about it—bring in some backup on this one.

So at dinner last night, I tried to bring it up. When I saw that Mom had her sweater on backward and could barely keep her eyes open, I knew she wouldn't be much help. (This author thing is really bringing her down.) But I figured DAD could give me some good advice, right?

Well, I gotta say, Dad was looking kind of frazzled too. See, he's been doing the cooking since Mom started writing, and it's really not one of Dad's best skills. When he said we were having leftover STEW for breakfast, I almost wished I were sitting at Ziggy Zombie's breakfast table. (I mean, I don't care for rotten-flesh sausages, but his mom makes a pretty tasty fried egg.)

Anyway, I told Dad I was worried about Sam. I said something was going on with him—that he might be spending too much time "studying." Well, that didn't work at all. See, parents don't really think there's such a thing as "too much studying."

So I tried something different. I said Sam was acting like he had some HUGE secret. But Dad didn't pick up on that hint either. Maybe it was because Cammy wouldn't eat her leftover stew and was threatening to explode.

Anyway, I finally had to just come out and say
it: "Dad, I think Mrs. Collins has been running
experiments on Sam in a secret room off the
library."

Well, THAT got his attention. And Mom's too. Chloe
burst out laughing, Cate cracked a smile, and Cammy
even held off on blowing up for a moment, which I
appreciated.

Then Dad cleared his throat and gave me the classic
parent line: "Gerald, I find that hard to believe."

But the thing about Dad is, he usually backs me
up—eventually. He said I was a good friend to be
worried about Sam, and that maybe I should invite
Sam for a sleepover this weekend so that Dad could
see for himself how Sam was doing.

I thought that was a GREAT idea. But Mom sure
didn't. Her eyes got all wild, and she said we

couldn't POSSIBLY _host a sleepover when she had_ only NINE _more days to finish her mystery._

"Yeah, how's that working out for you?" I asked. It shot out of my mouth like a rocket before I could shut the thing down.

Well, Mom didn't appreciate my tone of voice. She said she could use a little more support around here. She actually looked like she was going to cry.

But what about SAM??? I wanted to holler.

That's when Dad suggested that maybe I have a sleepover at Sam's house, and that he'd be happy to call Sam's parents and arrange it. So that was that. Mom settled down, Cammy ate her stew, and I went back to my room.

Now I'm trying to figure out what kind of detective work I can do at Sam's house this weekend. If Sam won't tell me what's going on in Room 117, are there OTHER ways I can find out?

There's gonna have to be. This may be my toughest detective work yet. But I am NOT going to let that sorry slime down.

DAY 22: SATURDAY

So I went to Sam's for a sleepover this morning. And I learned everything I need to know. EVERYTHING.

At first, Sam seemed normal. I mean, when I showed up, he was out on his trampoline. Sam's a bouncy guy, and he's got the biggest, best tramp you've ever seen. I got on there with him, and I watched his every move. He seemed all jolly and happy—same old slime.

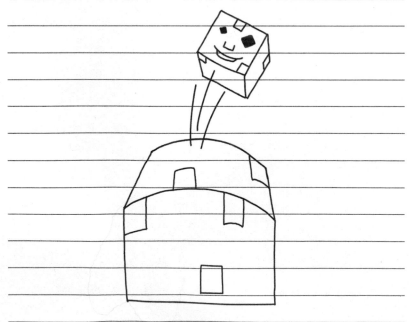

But as soon as we went inside, I KNEW something was up. Sam's bedroom is usually a slimy mess. But you know what? There wasn't a book or slimeball out of place. Sam said he was keeping it tidy to "help him study more."

There it was again—the studying thing. He had this whole desk set up with books in a neat little pile and a torch lamp. But that wasn't the WEIRDEST thing that I saw at Sam's. Nope, that came next.

See, there's nothing Sam loves more than his cat, Moo. Usually when I'm at his house, I have to witness these disgusting love sessions. Sam gets all smoochy with Moo, or shares his food with her, or picks her up and dances with her.

Anyway, when Moo wound her way into the bedroom and started rubbing up against Sam, I figured he'd scoop her up and give her a big wet smooch. But he didn't. He bounced backward. HUH?

Then Sam's mom hurried in and shooed Moo out—toward the bedroom that belongs to Sam's little brothers. "Go play with the boys," Mrs. Slime said to Moo. "Don't bother Sam."

BOTHER Sam? I must have scrunched up my face or something, because Mrs. Slime told me that Sam had suddenly started sneezing whenever Moo came around.

Sure enough, at that exact moment, Sam sneezed, and a sticky gob of slime landed on my cheek. That was pretty traumatic, let me tell you. But I barely noticed it, because I had just realized something:

This was NOT Sam.

Mrs. Collins must have done something with the old Sam and replaced him with this new creation.

This FRANKEN-slime who DIDN'T love cats. Who was ALLERGIC to cats. Who only wanted to STUDY!

Suddenly, I had to get out of there. I couldn't stand the sight of this new Sam—this fake Sam. So I told him I had homework of my own to do—that I'd just remembered a newspaper article that was due on Tuesday.

And you know what? I wasn't even lying. Because when a creep makes a discovery this big, he HAS to tell the world about it—or at least tell all of Mob Middle School. Someone has to put a stop to Mrs. Collins's scientific experiments.

I've decided that if no one at school listens to me, I'll send my article straight to the CREEPER CHRONICLE. It's time to tell the truth about what's going on around here.

My buddy Sam's life depends on it.

I only hope I'm not too late . . .

THE TRUTH ABOUT ROOM 117

By Gerald Creeper Jr.

Maybe some of you have noticed that Room 117 is ALWAYS locked. I sure did. And after very ~~exhausting~~ exhaustive research, I've deduced why.

Something's going on in that room that the teachers here at Mob Middle School DON'T want you to know about. (At least one teacher anyway.) But I'll let the facts speak for themselves:

- Fact 1. Mrs. Collins has been doing scientific experiments in that room.

- Fact 2. She gets in through a secret portal, hidden by a painting.

- Fact 3: One of her victims is our beloved Sam Sebastian Slime. (Sam, a lifelong cat lover, has suddenly developed an allergy to cats. And—GASP—a love for studying!)

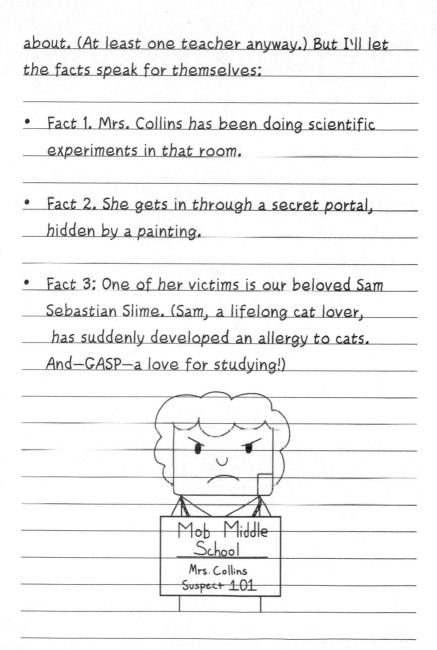

Mob Middle School
Mrs. Collins
Suspect 101

How many other victims are there? What is Mrs. Collins's evil plan? To turn every mob here at Mob Middle School into a PERFECT student?

The time has come to put an end to this madness. Let's show the teachers of Mob Middle School that WE WILL NOT STAND FOR IT.

Signed,

Gerald Creeper Jr., Lead Investigator
Ziggy Zombie, Assistant Investigator

DAY 24: MONDAY

I'm doing it—I'm turning in my newspaper article
TONIGHT. News this big HAS to be shared.

I even gave Ziggy part of the credit for cracking
this case. I think he'll appreciate that. (And if this
thing doesn't go over well, at least I won't go down
alone.)

Anyway, I'm going to give the article to Mr. Zane
on the sly. Because even though he's not my
favorite teacher, he seems like a pretty honest

guy. And we're gonna need some help busting Mrs. Collins.

If I'm wrong about Mr. Zane—or if ANYTHING happens to me—please send a copy of my newspaper article to the CREEPER CHRONICLE.

Oh, and look after Sticky.

And tell Mom and Dad that I'm sorry, but there comes a time in every creeper's life when he just has to stand up for what's right.

DAY 25: TUESDAY

WHAT does a creeper have to DO to get a grown-up to LISTEN around here?

I tried, I REALLY did. I gave Mr. Zane my article last night, and he read it on the spot. But instead of congratulating me for uncovering a secret and

dangerous operation at Mob Middle School, he
pulled me into his office.

At first, I thought he was trying to protect me—
like put me in a witness protection program or
something. I've heard about things like that, where
mobs who point the finger at criminals get sent
to different parts of the Overworld and live in

disguise. That way, the criminals can't hunt them down and blow them up or anything.

Well, let's just say that's NOT what Mr. Zane was doing. I figured it out as soon as he picked up his phone and called Dad. Fifteen minutes later, Dad showed up and walked me home.

When I tried to tell Dad what had happened—about the cobweb in Mrs. Collins's hair and the fact that Sam was sneezing all over Moo—he just stopped me and said, "Gerald, I'm afraid your mom and I have been neglecting you."

WHY do parents always DO that? They think everything is about them. Like when you do well in school, they take credit for it. And when you do something bad, they think they somehow RUINED you with their parenting.

Anyway, Dad thinks that I MADE UP the whole newspaper story to get attention. SERIOUSLY???

I was afraid Mom would think the same thing—that she'd meet me at the door in tears and tell me how

SORRY she was for caring more about her mystery novel than me. (Mom can be kind of dramatic sometimes.) But she didn't. She must have been out in her chicken coop.

When Dad asked if I wanted hot cocoa, I told him NO. I said I was going to my room and I wasn't going to eat or drink another thing until someone BELIEVED me.

I guess I can be kind of dramatic sometimes, too. But when a creeper takes a stand, he's gotta see it through.

DAY 25: TUESDAY (CONTINUED)

So I just figured out what a creeper's gotta do to get mobs to listen. I guess he's gotta blow his top and MAKE SOME NOISE.

See, Chloe barged into my room the minute she got home from school. She demanded to know what had happened with Mr. Zane. I guess there were rumors going around that I'd gotten expelled or something.

Anyway, I told Chloe that I'd given Mr. Zane my article—the one about Sam and Mrs. Collins. She gave me her sad little smirk, the one that says, "You're such a loser, Gerald. I'm embarrassed to call you my brother."

So when she came back a few minutes later to say something VERY WEIRD was happening in her closet,

I wasn't all that inclined to help her. I mean, why should I?

But I guess the detective in me won out. I guess I was tired of all the mysteries I couldn't solve. Maybe I couldn't bust Mrs. Collins in her Franken-slime science lab, but I could at LEAST solve The Case of Chloe's Creepy Closet.

The Case of Chloe's Creepy Closet

By Gerald Creeper Jr.

So I followed her in. But this time, we didn't
hear tapping. We heard CRYING. Whatever mob or
monster was on the other side of that "portal," it
wasn't a very happy one.

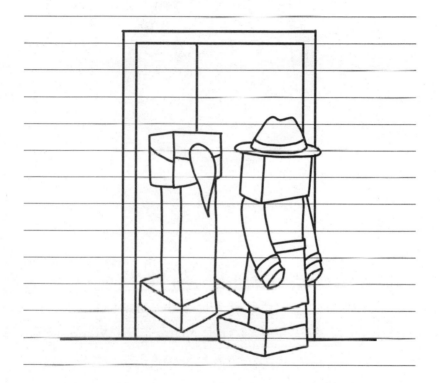

I started looking for clues. I pulled out my
magnifying glass. I tried to think of every tip I'd
ever gotten from the Sherlock Bones books. And

the whole time, Chloe just watched me with that smirk on her face.

Well, suddenly, I was pretty sure I knew how that mob on the other side of the wall felt—trapped, with no way out. While I stood there, listening to all that blubbering, something started BUBBLING inside of ME.

It fizzed and popped and hissed. It boiled over like mushroom stew in a pot three sizes too small.

I suddenly got hot and sweaty. And before I could tell Chloe to look out . . .

I BLEW.

For just a second, I felt better. Blowing up is like that—you get all the bad feelings out, once and for all. But after the gunpowder cleared, I saw the hole in Chloe's wall—and the mob that was hiding behind it.

MOM.

She must have been sitting at a desk, because
there were splinters of wood scattered all around.
And her laptop was SMOKING.

Well, I thought Mom would see her ruined laptop
and go all zombie pigwoman on me. But she didn't.
She just said in a tiny voice, "You found me."

Turns out, Mom had a secret room of her own—an unused closet hidden behind the dresser in my parents' bedroom. When the chicken coop office didn't really pan out, Mom turned this closet into an office. It was quiet. And private.

But now? It was ruined.

I must have apologized to Mom a gazillion times.

But you know what she said? She said it was probably
for the best. She said she was still working on
chapter one of her book, and that it was so boring,
even SHE fell asleep whenever she read it.

Anyway, Mom said that maybe she and I could both
get a good day's sleep for once. And she went right
to bed.

But me? Not so much. Because I may have blown open the Case of Chloe's Creepy Closet, but I still haven't convinced anyone about what's going on in Room 117. I've been banished from school, but SAM is still there.

Who's going to save him from Mrs. Collins now?

DAY 26: WEDNESDAY

Well, Mom and I have a new favorite saying: "You can't judge a book by its cover." Or a room by its door. Or a librarian by the cobweb in her hair. Something like that.

See, I got called BACK to school last night—by Mrs. Collins herself.

At first, I gotta say, I was scared. I mean, what did SHE want with ME? Was she going to experiment on ME, too? Was I going to come out of Room 117 a changed dude, just a shadow of the creeper I used to be?

I didn't want to go—until Mom said she'd go with me. Now I know Mom isn't exactly the toughest mob in the Overworld. But she can be fierce when she wants to be—like if someone messes with one of her chickens, or with one of her kids.

So with Mom by my side, we crept off to Mob Middle School. Mrs. Collins met us in the library, and Mr. Zane was there too.

You know what Mrs. Collins said first? She said SORRY. She told me she didn't blame me for writing that article about her, because she actually DID have a secret.

When she asked if I wanted to see Room 117, I froze up. Seriously. I felt like a pit of hot lava that someone had just poured water over—like I'd turned into this giant block of obsidian.

But Mom said it was okay—that she'd go, too. So before I knew it, I was following Mom and Mrs. Collins behind that painting, through that door, and into that mysterious room.

The first thing I saw were bookshelves—LOTS of them. But in the middle of the shelves was something I HADN'T seen before. I thought it was a furnace, but Mrs. Collins told me it was an "enchantment table."

She explained that it was really old, and that she'd discovered it this year, and that she'd been trying to see if she could get it to work.

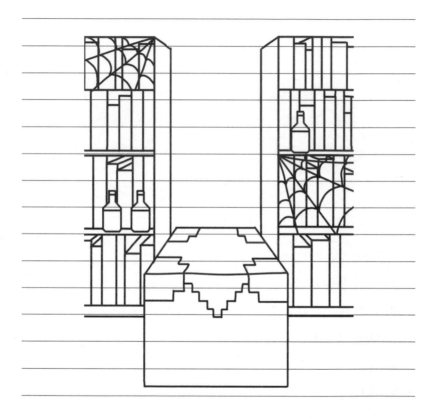

If she COULD make it work, she said, we could all learn how to do enchantments. I guess they're kind of like potions, but anyone can do them—not just witches.

Well, heck YES, I wanted to say—sign me up! But then I thought of Sam. Was SAM learning how to do enchantments? Is THAT why he'd been coming into this room?

I asked Mrs. Collins about Sam, but she just laughed. She said Sam had been kind enough to keep her secret, but that NO, he hadn't been coming to the room to do enchantments. She said I should probably ask HIM what he's been doing in that room—that maybe now he will tell me.

Well, I'm not so sure about that. I mean, the slime has been so slippery and secretive. Why would he suddenly tell me his secret now? The fake Sam that I imagined in my head over the last week or so sure wouldn't.

But I'm really hoping the REAL Sam will.

DAY 27: THURSDAY

I once lost my lucky mushroom. It's this petrified thing that my buddy Cash Creeper gave me before he moved away. And when I found it again under my bed, I felt like I'd just discovered a cave filled with emeralds. Like I was the luckiest creep in the Overworld.

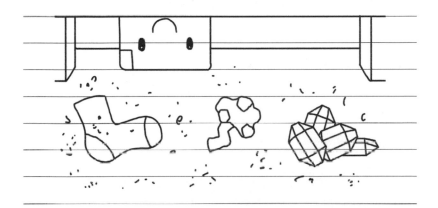

That's how I felt after hanging out with Sam this morning. See, it turns out, he's NOT a Franken-slime. He's MY slime—my best friend anyway.

When I told him about my meeting with Mrs. Collins, he let out this GINORMOUS sigh. He looked SO relieved, like I'd just lifted a giant block of obsidian off his shoulders.

I guess it's been really hard on Sam keeping Mrs. Collins's secret about the enchantment table. And when he found out I KNEW, then his other secrets poured right out of his mouth, too.

Secrets Secrets Secrets Secrets Secrets Secrets Secrets Secrets Secrets Secrets

Sam said _he hadn't just been studying on_ Wednesdays and Fridays after school. He'd been seeing a TUTOR. In Room 117.

A tutor? Well, why in the Overworld hadn't he just SAID so, I asked.

Sam got all weepy and puddle-like and said _he was_ embarrassed.

Because YOU'RE so good at school.

MOI? I mean, I'm pretty good at math and art. But I reminded Sam that he was WAY better at science.

179

And that I'd just gotten kicked off the newspaper staff and practically expelled from school.

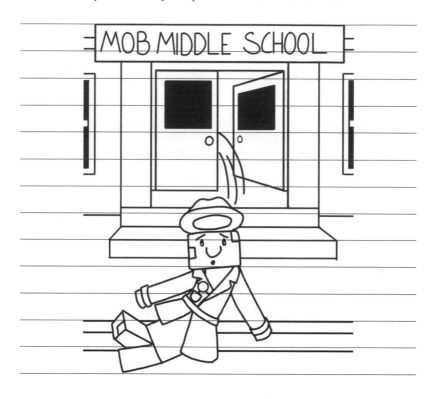

Well, that made him smile. And suddenly, Sam and I were back to good.

Especially when he pulled out his Cat Cam and showed me a video of him and Moo. I guess Sam's mom finally got him some allergy medicine, so he and his favorite critter are back to good, too. I didn't even mind the part of the video where Sam and Moo shared a hot chocolate. (Well, Moo licked off the whipped cream topping anyway.)

So everything is finally back to NORMAL around here. Well, except for the fact that I've decided to take Whisper Witch up on her offer to help me write a newspaper article.

Mrs. Collins asked me to cover a new story, and I really want to get it right. So Whisper Witch is coming over this weekend to FACT-check my article.

I guess I'd better get busy writing . . .

DAY 30: SUNDAY

I worked hard on this article, so you can imagine the happy dance I did when Whisper said it was good. REALLY good, she said.

I mean, I DID do most of the work. But I'm happy to give her credit, too. Because every good investigative reporter needs a sidekick.

Anyway, Dad read the article and said I might have a future as a writer, just like Mom. But Mom said she's pretty much done with all that. She's going to donate her Agatha Crispy books to my school library (which is good—we need a whole lot more mysteries and a whole lot fewer FACTS OF LIFE books!).

Oh, and Mom also decided to join a painting class. She wants to hang a painting in front of the hole I blew through the back of Chloe's closet. I guess Mom was inspired by the whole "painting in the library" thing at school.

Maybe there's no portal behind Chloe's wall, but Mom thinks they should keep the secret room—a place any of us can go when we need a little privacy.

As for me, I guess I've got a new plan too. See, there's this new extracurricular coming to Mob Middle School. Whisper Witch might join, too. Like I said, the girl signs up for pretty much everything. But you know what? That's okay by me.

MOB MIDDLE SCHOOL OBSERVER

AN "ENCHANTING" EXTRACURRICULAR
By Gerald Creeper Jr. and Whisper Witch

Sore from sprinting? Tired of strategically exploding? Not exactly LOVING llama riding? Well, join the club! The ENCHANTMENT CLUB, that is.

Yup, you heard it right, folks. Mrs. Collins is starting a new class in Room 117. She's dusting off the cobwebs, unlocking the door, and showing off Mob Middle School's very own enchantment table.

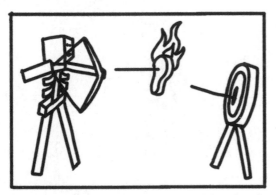

Check out the coolest BOOKS you'll ever read—the ENCHANTED kind. Create an enchanted HELMET that helps you breathe underwater.

Enchanted ARROWS that can set things on fire. (Burnt pork chops, anyone?)

Enchanted ARMOR that lets you walk through flames. (Field trip to the Nether? Sign us up!)

You heard it here first: The Enchantment Club is coming to Mob Middle School. Join us in Room 117 on Fridays after school.

Oh, and remember, kids: NEVER judge a book by its cover. There might be something "enchanting" hiding inside!

DON'T MISS ANY OF GERALD CREEPER JR.'S HILARIOUS ADVENTURES!

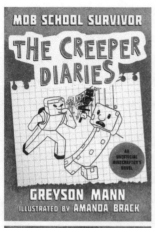

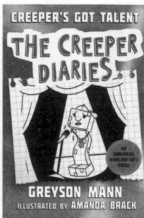

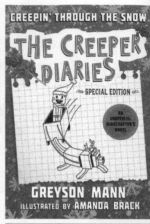

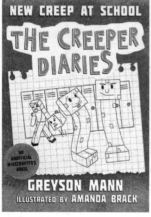

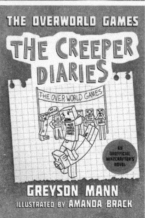

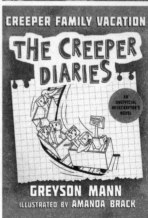

Sky Pony Press
New York